Publisher's Cataloging-in-Publication Data
Anand, Smiti.
Angelina and the smelly monster / Smiti Anand [and] Dan Ungureanu.
pages cm
ISBN 978-0-9862932-0-7

1. Monsters — Fiction.

2. Baths — Fiction.

3. Cleanliness — Fiction.

4. Friendship — Juvenile fiction.

I. Ungureanu, Dan. II. Title.
PZ7.A51836 An 2015   [Fic] — dc23   2014922582

Edited by: G. Parthasarathy

First Edition
Printed in China

ANGELiNA
and The Smelly Monster

by Smiti Anand & illustrated by Dan Ungureanu

Angelina lived in a big house in a small bedroom with a very small bear named Teddy.

The two of them had tea parties,

played hide and seek,

and ran around outside.

They did everything together. Teddy was Angelina's best friend.

One night, Angelina jumped into bed and Teddy slipped out of her hand.

Teddy landed under the bed before Angelina could catch him.

Angelina couldn't see Teddy, but she smelled something very stinky under the bed.
There was a monster under the bed!

Angelina decided to be brave.

"Hi Monster! My name is Angelina.
 What's your name?" she said.

"My name is Lester," growled the monster.

"Lester, why did you take Teddy?"
she asked.

"All the other monsters tease me. They call me Lester the smelly monster. They make me feel bad. Teddy makes me feel better," Lester said. "Lester, you don't sound like a bad monster. Come out and I'll help you."

Angelina was surprised that Lester wasn't scary.
He was just very, very, very dirty.

Lester snorted, "How could YOU help me?"
"You are only a little girl, Angelina."

"Hey! I'm smart and brave. I can fix any problem. You are the smelly monster, you need my help,"Angelina said angrily.

Lester hugged Teddy as he sobbed."You are right, Angelina."

Angelina felt bad for Lester.

"Don't worry Lester. I can help you smell better if you give Teddy back to me."

Lester hugged Teddy. "Thank you Teddy for helping me feel better," Lester said.

Lester gently gave Teddy back to Angelina. Angelina held Teddy safely in her arms.

Angelina walked Lester
down the hall.

"What is this place?"
Lester asked.

"This is a bathroom. We
come here to get clean. I
think it will help you smell
better too," Angelina said.

Lester gasped, "Oh no! It's a monster."

Angelina laughed. "That's you, Lester."

"That's me?" Lester asked.
"That's a mirror. It shows you
what you look like," Angelina
said.

"Climb in Lester. This is a bathtub. It will help you smell better."

"Lester, now you will take a bath. Tell me if the water is too cold or hot," Angelina said.

"Angelina, don't worry. My fur keeps me just right," Lester said proudly.

Angelina showed Lester how to soap up his fur and spray it all off.

Mud, bugs, and old banana peels plopped out of his fur!

"Lester, your fur is clean!"

Lester grinned.

Angelina saw his teeth were **BLACK!**

"Lester, if you brush your teeth, you will smell even better."

"Put the toothbrush in your mouth," Angelina said. Lester put it all the way in his mouth.

"No, No, on your TEETH, Lester!"

Angelina brushed Lester's big teeth very carefully.

"Lester, you can spit if you need to." Lester spit all over the floor.

"Oh NO! In the SINK!" Angelina said quickly.

It was too late. There were puddles everywhere.

Yikes! There were still things on his teeth.

"Lester, brushing is not enough."

Angelina gently flossed his teeth.

Lester swished around the mouthwash that Angelina gave him.

Finally, they were **DONE!**

"Lester, you look and smell great," Angelina said proudly.

"Thank you so much for helping me and being my friends. Now I can go back home smelling good," Lester said happily.

"Ok Lester! Come back soon," Angelina said.

Lester smiled and hugged them both before he said goodbye.

Angelina and Teddy had become friends with a monster. They weren't worried about the monster goop all around. They knew they could handle anything. If only Lester could clean. Angelina laughed. Maybe next time...

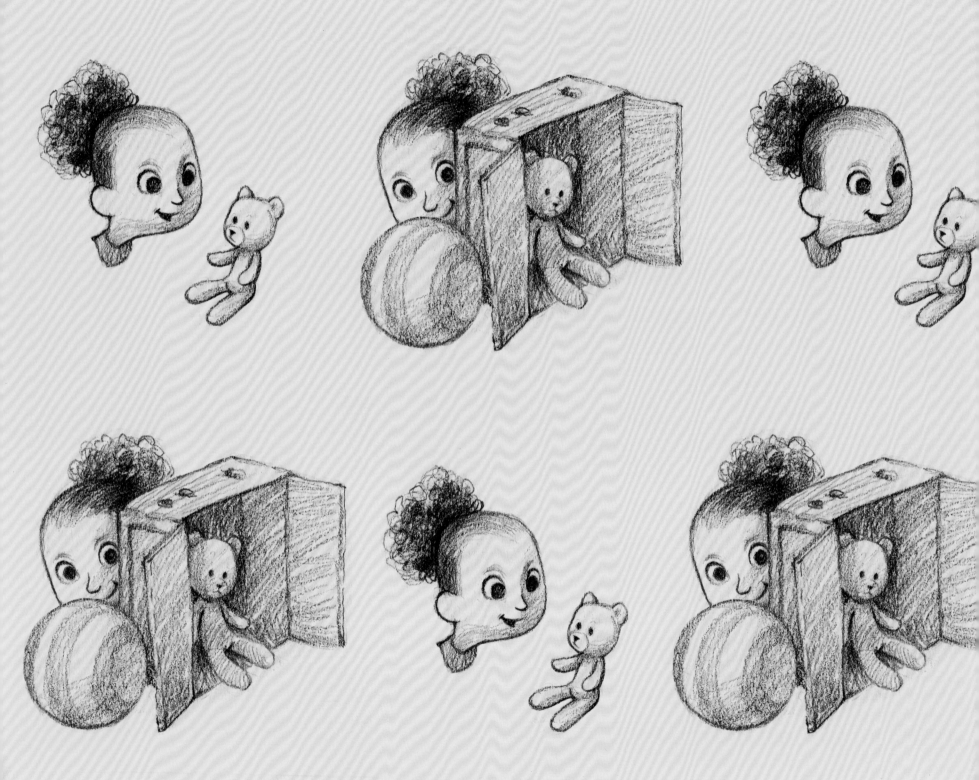

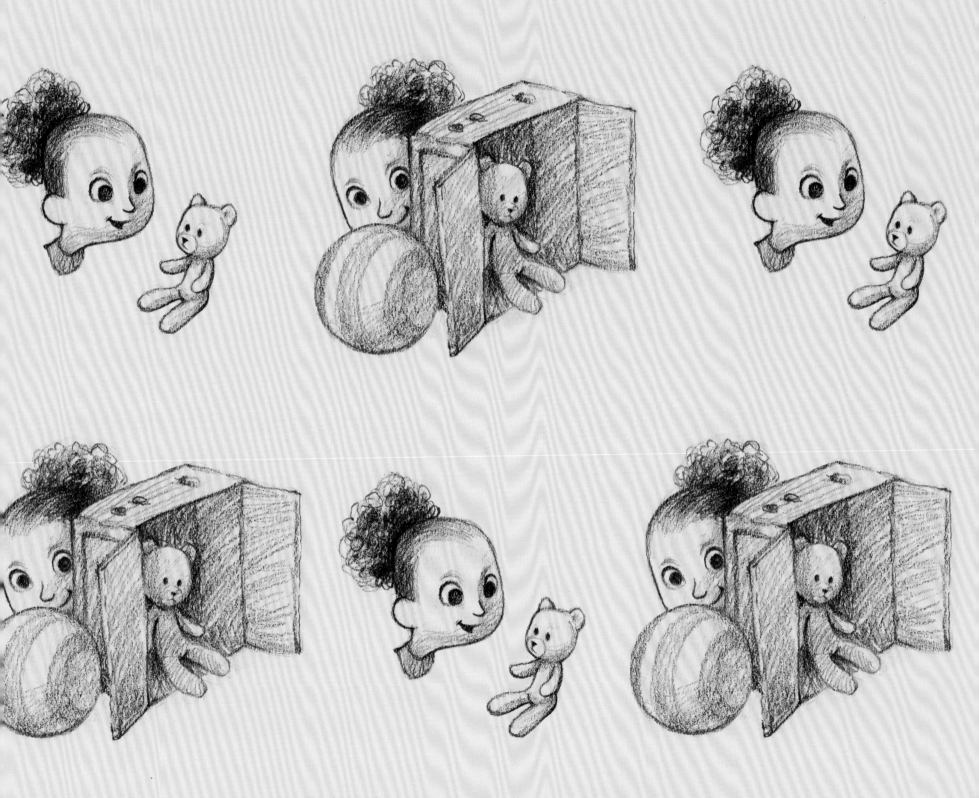

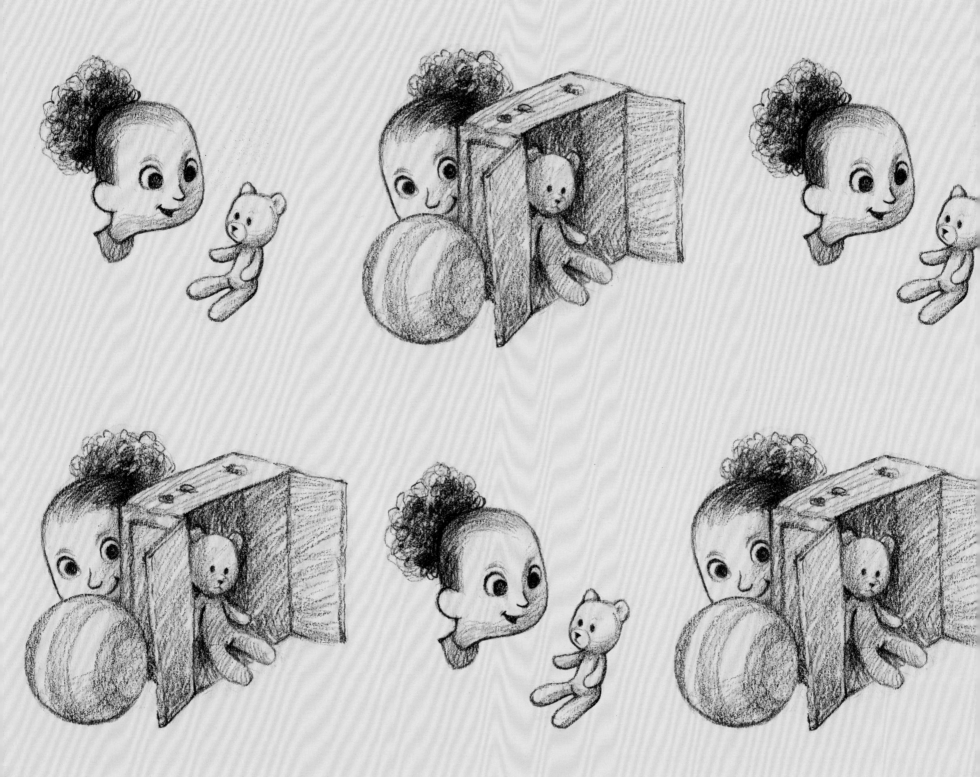